Classic Pages

Marigold Garden

金盏花花园

[英] 凯特·格林威（Kate Greenaway） 著/绘

繁多 译

向凯特·格林威致敬

辽宁人民出版社

You little girl,
You little boy,
With wondering eyes
That kindly look.
In honour of
Two noble names
I send the offering
Of this book.

小女孩儿，
小男孩儿，
睁大你好奇的双眼认真读。
为纪念两个高贵的名字，
我献上这本插画给你看。

CONTENTS

SUSAN BLUE ··· 010

BLUE SHOES ··· 012

STREET SHOW ·· 014

TO THE SUN DOOR ·· 016

THE DAISIES ·· 020

THE DANCING FAMILY ·· 022

GOING TO SEE GRANDMAMMA ···································· 026

WISHES ··· 030

FIRST ARRIVALS ··· 032

WHEN WE WENT OUT WITH GRANDMAMMA ················· 036

TO MYSTERY LAND ··· 042

FROM MARKET ··· 046

LITTLE PHILLIS ··· 048

THE FOUR PRINCESSES ·· 052

目录

苏珊·布卢 …………………………………… 011

小小蓝鞋子 …………………………………… 013

街头秀 ………………………………………… 015

致太阳门 ……………………………………… 017

雏菊 …………………………………………… 021

跳舞家族 ……………………………………… 023

去看奶奶 ……………………………………… 027

愿望 …………………………………………… 031

第一个到达的人 ……………………………… 033

和奶奶一起散步 ……………………………… 037

去神奇岛 ……………………………………… 043

赶集归来 ……………………………………… 047

小菲莉斯 ……………………………………… 049

四位公主 ……………………………………… 053

WHEN YOU AND I GROW UP	056
IN AN APPLE TREE	058
THE WEDDING BELLS	060
THE LITTLE LONDON GIRL	062
TO BABY	066
WILLY AND HIS SISTER	068
AT SCHOOL	074
HAPPY DAYS	076
THE LITTLE QUEEN'S COMING	080
ON THE WALL TOP	084
TIP-A-TOE	088
MAMMAS AND BABIES	090
MY LITTLE GIRLIE	096
THE CATS HAVE COME TO TEA	100
THE TEA PARTY	104
UNDER ROSE ARCHES	106
A GENTEEL FAMILY	110
BABY MINE	116
LITTLE GIRLS AND LITTLE LAMBS	118

当你和我长大	057
苹果树上	059
婚礼的钟声	061
伦敦小姑娘	063
致宝宝	067
威利和他的姐姐	069
在学校	075
欢乐时光	077
小女王驾到	081
走在城墙上	085
踮起脚尖	089
妈妈们和孩子们	091
我的小姑娘	097
猫咪来喝茶	101
茶话会	105
在玫瑰廊下	107
教养之家	111
我的宝贝	117
小姑娘和小羔羊	119

FROM WONDER WORLD	122
CHILD'S SONG	126
MISS MOLLY AND THE LITTLE FISHES	128
THE LITTLE JUMPING GIRLS	132
RING-A-RING	136
ON THE BRIDGE	138
BALL	142

来自奇幻的国度 …………………………………… 123

儿歌 ……………………………………………… 127

茉莉小姐和小鱼儿 ……………………………… 129

小女孩，蹦蹦跳 ………………………………… 133

转圆圈 …………………………………………… 137

在桥上 …………………………………………… 139

抛球 ……………………………………………… 143

译后记 …………………………………………… 146

SUSAN BLUE

OH, Susan Blue,

How do you do?

Please may I go for a walk with you?

Where shall we go?

Oh, I know —

Down in the meadow where the cowslips grow!

苏珊·布卢

哦，苏珊·布卢，
最近可好呀？
我能否请你一起去散步？
去哪里呀？
哦，我知道——
去那片长满野樱草的草地吧！

BLUE SHOES

LITTLE Blue Shoes
Mustn't go
Very far alone, you know.
Else she'll fall down,
Or, lose her way,
Fancy — what
Would mamma say?
Better put her little hand
Under sister's wise command.
When she's a little older grown,
Blue Shoes may go quite alone.

小小蓝鞋子

要知道
穿小蓝鞋子的姑娘
不会一个人走太远,
或者,她会跌倒,
或者,她迷了路,
范茜——妈妈怎么说的?
请用姐姐的智慧
将妹妹的手牵住。
等她再长大一些,
穿着小蓝鞋子,
妹妹自己就能走路。

STREET SHOW

PUFF, puff, puff. How the trumpets blow.

All you little boys and girls come and see the show.

One — two — three, the Cat runs up the tree,

But the little Bird he flies away —

"She hasn't got me!"

街头秀

叭,叭,叭!小喇叭吹响啦,
男孩儿和女孩儿,快过来看秀。
一、二、三——大猫蹿上树,
小鸟却飞走啦,
"哈、哈、哈,大猫没把我逮住!"

TO THE SUN DOOR

THEY saw it rise in the morning;
    They saw it set at night.
And they longed to go and see it,
    Ah! If they only might.

致太阳门

他们看见太阳早上升起,
他们瞧见太阳傍晚落去。
如果可以的话,
他们渴望去看太阳。

The little soft white clouds heard them,
And stepped from out of the blue;
And each laid a little child softly
Upon its bosom of dew.

And they carried them higher and higher,
And they nothing knew any more
Until they were standing waiting
In front of the round gold door.

And they knocked, and railed, and entreated,
Whoever should be within;
Until all to no purpose, for no one
Would hearken to let them in.

柔软的白云听到了他们的期许，
从蓝天中探出脸庞；
将小孩儿温柔地
放在挂满露珠的云朵上。

云朵载着孩子们越升越高，
他们一脸迷惘，
直到站在那圆圆的
金色的大门旁。

孩子们敲呀，叫啊，最后乞求，
谁在里面呢？能否开下大门？
但里面毫无回应，
更没人听到，请他们进门。

THE DAISIES

YOU very fine Miss Molly,
What will the daisies say,
If you carry home so many
Of their little friends today?

Perhaps you take a sister,
Perhaps you take a brother,
Or two little daisies who,
Were fond of one another.

雏菊

善良的莫莉小姐呀,
听听雏菊会咋说,
今天你摘了好多要带回家?
可它们都是彼此的好朋友。

你摘的也许是它们的姐妹,
你摘的也许是它们的兄弟,
或许摘下的两小朵
正是互相喜欢的小伙伴。

THE DANCING FAMILY

PRAY let me introduce you to
 This little dancing family;
For morning, afternoon, and night
 They danced away so happily.

They twirled round about,
 And they turned their toes out;
The people wondered what the noise
 Could all be about.

跳舞家族

请允许我给你们介绍:
这个小小的舞蹈家族,
从清晨、中午到夜晚,
他们一直在乐舞翩翩。

他们翩翩旋转,
他们脚尖踮起;
邻居们都很纳闷,
为何舞蹈的噪声终不停息?

They danced from early morning,
Till very late at night,
Both in-doors and out-of-doors,
With very great delight.

And every sort of dance they knew,
From every country far away;
And so it was no wonder that
They should keep dancing all the day.

So dancing — dancing — dancing,
In sunshine or in rain;
And when they all left off,
Why then — they all began again.

他们从破晓清晨
跳到半夜三更,
从室内跳到屋外,
他们总跳得那么欢快。

他们通晓每一种舞步,
哪怕它来自遥远的国度;
所以毫无疑问,
他们整日整夜地舞蹈,从不歇步。

所以,跳吧,跳吧,跳吧,
不管日晒和下雨。
一曲终了人不散,
新乐响来舞再起。

GOING TO SEE GRANDMAMMA

LITTLE Molly and Damon
Are walking so far,
For they're going to see
Their kind Grandmamma.

去看奶奶

小莫莉和小达蒙
走的路会很远,
因为他们要去
看望慈祥的奶奶。

And they very well know,
When they get there she'll take
From out of her cupboard
Some very nice cake.

And into her garden
They know they may run,
And pick some red currants,
And have lots of fun.

So Damon to doggie
Says, "How do you?"
And asks his mamma
If he may not go too.

他们都知道，
到了奶奶家她就会
从橱柜里拿出
喷喷香的蛋糕。

他们会冲进奶奶的花园
连跑带跳，
会去摘红醋栗子，
欢天喜地，放声尖叫。

达蒙转向小狗狗，
说："伙计，你好！"
然后征求妈妈，
狗狗是否可以一同前往。

WISHES

OH, if you were a little boy,
And I was a little girl —
Why you would have some whiskers grow,
And then my hair would curl.

Ah! If I could have whiskers grow,
I'd let you have my curls;
But what's the use of wishing it —
Boys never can be girls.

愿望

哦，如果你是小男孩儿，
　而我是小女孩儿，
　　那么你会长胡子，
　而我就会留卷发。

啊！如果我能长出胡子，
　我会让你的头发也打卷；
　　可愿望终归是愿望，
男孩儿永远变不成女孩儿。

FIRST ARRIVALS

IT is a Party, do you know?
And there they sit, all in a row,
Waiting till the others come,
To begin to have some fun.

Hark! The bell rings sharp and clear.
Other little friends appear;
And no longer all alone
They begin to feel at home.

第一个到达的人

知道吗,开晚会啦!
　大家坐成一排,
　等着其他人的到来,
　　开始举杯畅怀。

听!铃声响得多清脆呀,
　其他小朋友们来啦;
　大家都宾至如归,
　没人再觉得孤单。

To them a little hard is Fate,
Yet better early than too late;
Fancy getting there forlorn,
With the tea and cake all gone.

Wonder what they'll have for tea;
Hope the jam is strawberry.
Wonder what the dance and game;
Feel so very glad they came.

Very Happy may you be;
May you much enjoy your tea.

命运对他们有些残酷,
　　赶早不赶晚总没坏处;
不像范茜站在那里很孤独,
　　没有茶喝,没有蛋糕吃。

不知道他们会喝什么茶,
　　希望有甜甜的草莓果酱。
不知道会跳哪支舞,会做什么游戏;
　　只要大家都来就很欢喜。

祝大家玩得开心,
　　祝你喝茶喝得如意。

WHEN WE WENT OUT WITH GRANDMAMMA

WHEN we went out with Grandmamma—
Mamma said for a treat—
Oh, dear, how stiff we had to walk,
As we went down the street.

One on each side we had to go,
And never laugh or loll;
I carried Prim, her Spaniard dog
And Tom— her parasol.

和奶奶一起散步

我们和奶奶一起出门,
妈妈说要去请客吃饭;
哦,天哪,我们沿着大街往前走,
身姿笔直,走姿古板。

我们伴在奶奶左右,
不能大笑更不能牵拉头;
我抱着她的西班牙狗——普里姆,
而汤姆手握着她的阳伞。

If I looked right — if Tom looked left —
"Tom — Susan I'm ashamed;
And little Prim, I'm sure, is shocked,
To hear such naughties named."

She said we had no manners,
If we ever talked or sung;
"You should have seen," said Grandmamma,
"Me walk, when I was young."

She told us — oh, so often —
How little girls and boys,
In the good days when she was young,
Never made any noise.

如果我东张，汤姆西望，
"汤姆、苏珊让我丢脸失望；
我确信，小普里姆会吓一跳，
听到你们两个淘气包的名字被喊出。"

如果我们又聊又唱，
奶奶会说我们没有礼貌；
还会说道："你们应该知道，
我小的时候，散步的时候就散步。"

她常对我们讲起，
她小时候那些美好时光，
那时候的男孩儿女孩儿，
从来不叽叽喳喳。

She said they never wished then
To play — oh, no, indeed!
They learnt to sew and needlework,
Or else to write and read.

She said her mother never let
Her speak a word at meals;
"But now," said Grandmamma, "you'd think
That children's tongues had wheels."

"So fast they go — clack, clack, clack, clack;
Now listen well, I pray,
And let me see you both improve
From what I've said today."

她说他们从来不想着贪玩,
哦,从不!
他们只会学习纺织和做针线活,
要不就去写字和读书。

她说她的妈妈从不会允许
她在吃饭的时候说话;
"可是现在,"奶奶说,"你们要知道,
现在的孩子们满嘴跑火车。"

"满嘴火车跑得快——喀啦、喀啦、喀啦、喀啦;
现在请仔细听,我期待
从今天我说完,
我看看你们的进步到底有多大。"

TO MYSTERY LAND

OH, dear, how will it end?
Peggy and Susie how naughty you are.
You little know where you are,
Going so far, and so high,
Nearly up to the sky.
Perhaps it's a Giant who lives there,
And perhaps it's a lovely Princess.
But you very well know
You've no business to go;
You'll get yourselves into a mess.

去神奇岛

哦,天啊,还不快停下?
佩吉和苏茜你们可真淘气。
你们自己都不知爬到何处去,
爬得那么远,爬得那么高,
简直是要腾云驾雾爬上天!
也许那里住着一位巨人,
也许那里有可爱的公主。
但你们心里都一清二楚,
这些都和你们毫不相干;
你们却让自己乱作一团。

Oh, dear, I'm sure it is true:
Whatever on earth can it matter to you?
For you know it — oh, fie —
That it's naughty to pry
Into other's affairs —
Into other folks houses to go,
Where you know
You're not asked.
So you'd better come back,
While there's time, it is plain.
Go home — and be never
So naughty again.

哦，天啊，我确信无疑，
无论那里有什么与你们何干？
　你们也心知肚明——
　　窥探别人的隐私，
　　是多么的无礼；
　你们更心里有数——
　　私闯他人的领地，
　　是多么让人唾弃。
所以你们最好快回来！
　趁时间还来得及。
　回家去，永远不要
　　再那么淘气。

FROM MARKET

On who'll give us Posies,
And Garlands of Roses,
To twine round our heads so happy?
For here we come singing,
And here we come bringing
You many good wishes today.
From market — from market — from market —
We all come up from market.

赶集归来

谁愿意给我们送来花束，
还为我们戴上玫瑰花环，
盘在头顶让我们心生喜欢？
我们在此放声歌唱，
我们今日为你祝福。
赶集归来，赶集归来，赶集归来，
我们都刚刚赶集归来。

LITTLE PHILLIS

I am a very little girl.
I think that I've turned two;
And if you'd like to know my name,
I'll like to tell it you.

They always call me Baby,
But Phillis is my name.
No — no one ever gave it me;
I think it only came.

小菲莉斯

我是一个小女孩,
 我想我已经两岁了;
如果你想知道我叫啥,
 我很乐意告诉你。

他们总叫我"宝贝",
 可我的名字是菲莉斯。
这不是别人给我起的,
 我生来就叫这个名字。

I've got a pretty tulip
In my little flower-bed;
If you would like I'll give it you —
It's yellow, striped with red.

I've got a little kitten, but
I can't give that away.
She likes to play with me so much;
She's gone to sleep today.

And I've got a nice new dolly;
Shall I fetch her out to you?
She's got such pretty shoes on,
And her bonnet's trimmed with blue.

You'd like to take her home with you?
Oh, no, she mustn't go;
Goodbye — I want to run now,
And you walk alone so slow.

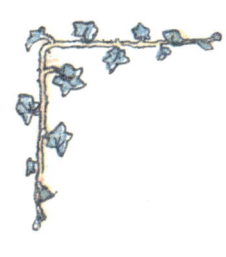

在我的小花床,
栽着漂亮的郁金香;
你若喜欢,我将它给你,
黄的花瓣,嵌着红的条条。

我养了一只小猫,
可我不能送给你。
她很喜欢和我一起玩;
她今天已经睡去。

我还有个好看的新娃娃,
要不把她抱出来给你看?
她脚蹬那双漂亮的鞋子,
头戴的帽檐镶着蓝花边。

你想要把她带回家吗?
哦!不,她绝不能去;
再见了,我要跑开了,
你一个人就慢慢走吧。

THE FOUR PRINCESSES

FOUR Princesses lived in a Green Tower —
A Bright Green Tower in the middle of the sea;
And no one could think — oh, no one could think —
Who the Four Princesses could be.

One looked to the North, and one to the South,
And one to the East, and one to the West;
They were all so pretty, so very pretty,
And you could not tell which was the prettiest.

四位公主

四位公主住在绿塔之上,
亮亮的绿塔矗立于海的中央;
没人知晓,哦!更没人猜到,
四位公主究竟来自何方。

一位望着北方,一位看着南方,
一位瞭向东方,一位探向西方;
她们多么美丽,多么漂亮,
无法说清谁是最靓丽的仙女。

Their curls were golden, their eyes were blue,
And their voices were sweet as a silvery bell;
And four white birds around them flew,
But where they came from — who could tell?

Oh, who could tell? For no one knew,
And not a word could you hear them say.
But the sound of their singing, like church bells ringing,
Would sweetly float as they passed away.

For under the sun, and under the stars,
They often sailed on the distant sea;
Then in their Green Tower and Roses bower
They lived again — a mystery.

她们长得金发碧眼,
她们的声音如银铃般甜美;
四只白鸟围着她们展翅飞翔,
但谁能说出——她们来自何方?

哦,谁能说出呢?因为没人知道,
至今还没人听到她们的只言片语。
但她们的歌声,宛如教堂的钟声响亮,
当她们逝去,那甜蜜的歌声依旧会在空中飘荡。

太阳之下,星空之下,
她们常常出没于海上,渐行渐远;
最后回到绿塔和玫瑰花房,
再次重生,续写传奇之王。

WHEN YOU AND I GROW UP

WHEN you and I
Grow up, Polly—
I mean that you and me,
Shall go sailing in a big ship
Right over all the sea.
We'll wait till we are older,
For if we went today,
You know that we might lose ourselves,
And never find the way.

当你和我长大

当你和我长大,
　波莉——
我是说你和我,
我们将乘艘大船远行,
　穿越整个海洋。
我们要等到自己长大,
因为如果我们现在就去,
　可能会迷失自我,
　永远找不到路返航。

IN AN APPLE TREE

In September, when the apples were red,

To Belinda I said,

"Would you like to go away

To Heaven, or stay

Here in this orchard full of trees

All your life?" And she said, "if you please

I'll stay here — where I know,

And the flowers grow."

苹果树上

苹果红了的九月,
我对贝琳达说:
"你愿意远走高飞去天堂,还是
一辈子守在这长满树的果园里?"
她说:"如果可以的话,
我要待在我熟悉的地方,
这里到处鲜花盛放。"

THE WEDDING BELLS

THE Wedding Bells were ringing,
And Monday was the day,
And all the little ladies
Where there so fresh and happy.

And up, up, up the steps they went,
The wedding fine to see;
And the Roses were all for the Bride,
So pretty, so pretty was she.

婚礼的钟声

婚礼的钟声敲响,
日子是周一,
所有的小伴娘,
个个神清气爽、喜气洋洋。

她们一步一步迈上台阶,
婚礼就该如此壮观的模样;
所有的玫瑰花都献给新娘,
她是那么的美丽漂亮。

THE LITTLE LONDON GIRL

IN my little Green House, quite content am I,
When the hot sun pours down from the sky;
For oh, I love the country — the beautiful country.
Who'd live in a London street when there's the country?

I live in a London street, then I long and long
To be the whole day the sweet Flowers among
Instead of tall chimney-pots up in the sky,
The joy of seeing Birds and Dragon Flies go by.

伦敦小姑娘

住在我绿色的小房里,我是多么满足舒爽,
　　即便炽热的阳光从天而降;
　　哦,我还是爱——这个美丽的村庄。
有了这样的村庄,谁愿意住在伦敦的大街上?

我住在伦敦的大街上,却不停不停地向往,
　　盼望整日能在花丛中徜徉,
　　厌倦了到处高耸入云的烟囱,
看到鸟儿和蜻蜓的起舞,不快才一扫而光。

At home I lie in bed, and cannot go to sleep,
For the sound of cart-wheels upon the hard street.
But here my eyes close up to no sound of anything
Except it is to hear the nightingales sing.

And then I see the Chickens and the Geese go walking,
I hear the Pigs and the Ducks all talking.
And the Red and the Spotted Cows they stare at me,
As if they wondered whoever I could be.

I see the little Lambs out with their mothers —
Such pretty little white young sisters and brothers.
Oh, I'll stay in the country, and make a daisy chain,
And never go back to London again.

在家里,我躺在床上无法入睡,
因为那碾过石板街的车轮嗒嗒作响。
但这儿,我闭上眼睛万籁俱寂,
只有夜莺的歌唱回荡在我的耳旁。

我看到鸡和鹅在散步,
我听到猪和鸭在聊天说话。
红牛和斑点牛盯着我看,
好像它们想知道我是谁。

我看到小羊羔跟着自己的妈妈出来徜徉,
羔羊小兄妹身着雪白衣裳是多么的漂亮!
哦,我要留在乡下,用雏菊做条项链,
再也不做伦敦城里的小姑娘!

TO BABY

OH, what shall my blue eyes go see?
Shall it be pretty Quack-Quack today?
Or the Peacock upon the Yew Tree?
Or the dear little white Lambs at play?
Say Baby.
For Baby is such a young Petsy,
And Baby is such a sweet Dear.
And Baby is growing quite old now—
She's just getting on for a year.

致宝宝

哦,我的蓝眼睛今天看什么好?
是要看小鸭子嘎嘎叫?
还是看紫杉树上的孔雀微笑?
或是看可爱的小羊羔玩耍嬉闹?
宝宝说了算!
因为宝宝太娇小,
宝宝真可爱。
宝宝长大啦,
就要满岁了。

WILLY AND HIS SISTER

威利和他的姐姐

Willy said to his sister,
"Please may I go with you?"
She said, "you must behave
Very nicely if you do."

"Please will you take me then
To look at the mill?"
"Yes," she said, "because you are
So very good — I will."

"The miller he is
So very white and kind;
And sprinkled all over
With the flour they grind."

"And the big heaps of corn
That lie upon the floor,
He will let me play with those,
I am quite sure."

威利问姐姐:
"我能和你一起去吗?"
姐姐回答说:
"要去,那你必须守规矩。"

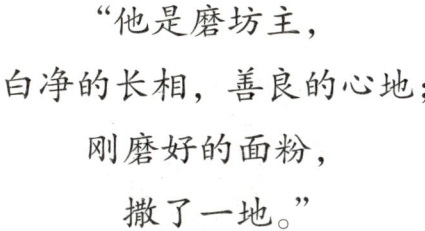

"那么能带我去
看看磨坊吗?"
"可以。"姐姐回答说,
"你要那么乖,我会很乐意。"

"他是磨坊主,
白净的长相,善良的心地;
刚磨好的面粉,
撒了一地。"

"堆积在地板上的
是一大堆的玉米。
他会让我在上面嬉戏,
这一点我确信无疑。"

"I like to hear the wheel
Make such a rushing sound,
And see the pretty water
Go round, and round, and round."

"So take me to the mill,
For then you shall see
What a very, very good boy
I really mean to be."

"我喜欢听磨坊水轮的转动声,
　吱吱嘎嘎,急促轰鸣,
　也喜欢看那潺潺的水流,
　转啊,转啊,转个不停。"

"所以带我去磨坊吧,
　那样你会看到,
　我真的是一个非常棒、
　非常乖的男儿郎。"

AT SCHOOL

FIVE little Girls, sitting on a form,
Five little Girls, with lessons to learn;
Five little Girls, who, I'm afraid,
Won't know them a bit when they have to be said.

For little eyes are given to look
Anywhere else than on their book;
And little thoughts are given to stray
Anywhere — ever so far away.

在学校

五个小女孩,坐成排,
五个小女孩,一起学;
五个小女孩,我还担着心,
可能还是一问三不知。

五双小眼睛四处张望,
望向书本之外的地方;
陷入遐想眼神迷惘,
思绪早已飘向远方。

HAPPY DAYS

"ARE you going next week to see Phillis and Pheebe?
Phillis on Monday will be just fourteen.
She says we shall all have our tea in the garden,
And afterwards have some nice games on the green."

"I wanted a new frock, but mother said, 'no,'
So I must be content with my old one you see.
But then white is so pretty, and kind Aunt Matilda
Has sent down a beautiful necklace for me."

欢乐时光

"你下周要去看菲莉斯和菲比吗?
菲莉斯星期一将满十四啦。
她邀请我们一起在花园里喝茶,
然后在草地上打几场漂亮的比赛。"

"我想要件新裙子,妈妈却说,'没有',
所以你瞧,我只能选件旧的穿上,
白色的这件很漂亮,多亏好心的玛蒂尔达姨妈,
她送了条漂亮的项链给我配搭。"

"Oh, yes, I am going, and Peggy is going,
And mother is making us new frocks to wear;
I shall have my red sash and my hat with pink ribbons —
I know all the girls will be smart who are there."

"And then, too, we're going to each take a nosegay —
The larger the better — for Phillis to say
That all her friends love her, and wish her so happy,
And bring her sweet flowers upon her birthday."

"And won't it be lovely, in beautiful sunshine,
The table spread under the great apple tree,
To see little Phillis — that dear little Phillis —
Look smiling all round as she pours out the tea!"

"哦,是的,我会去的,佩吉也去,
　　妈妈正在给我们赶做新裙子;
我将系上红肩带,帽子配上粉丝带,
　　我知道去那儿的女孩儿既聪明又漂亮。"

"对了,我们每个人还要捧束鲜花,
　　对菲莉斯来说,当然越大越好啦,
因为所有的朋友都爱她,祝她幸福,
　　在她生日当天为她送上鲜花。"

"多么美好的时光,相聚在明媚的阳光下,
　　茶桌摆放在高大的苹果树下,
瞧瞧小菲莉斯,亲爱的小菲莉斯,
　　一边为我们倒茶,一边满脸乐开了花!"

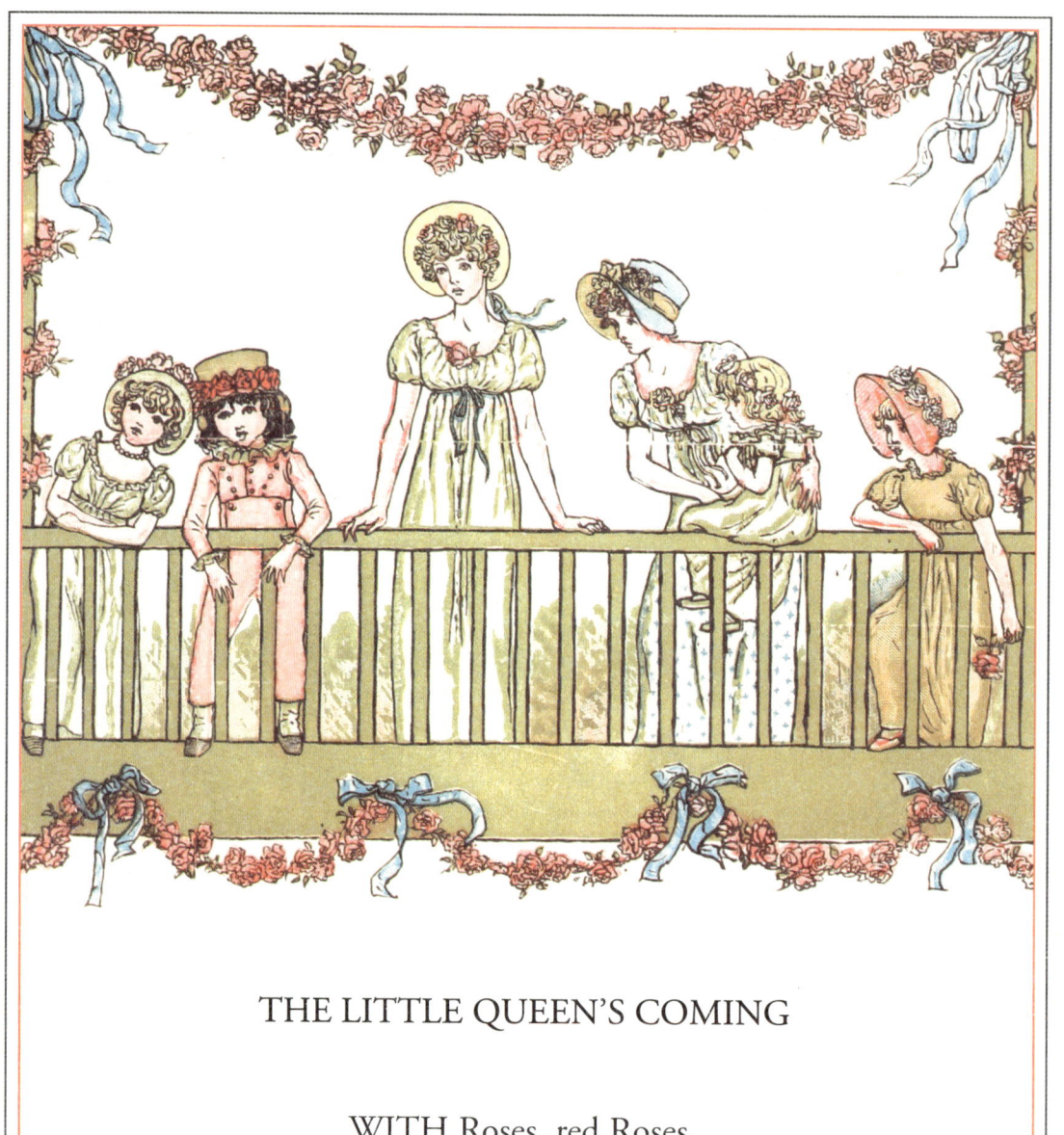

THE LITTLE QUEEN'S COMING

WITH Roses, red Roses,
We'll pelt her with Roses;
And Lilies, white Lilies, we'll drop at her feet;

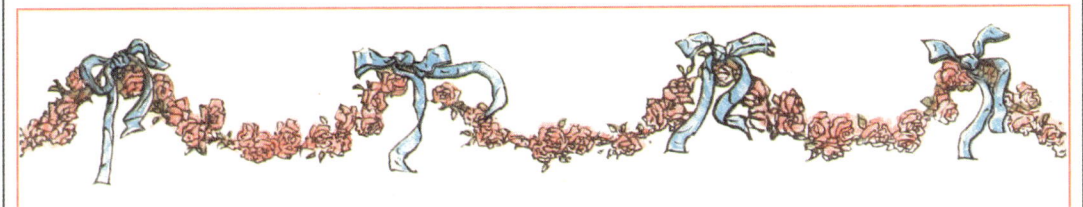

小女王驾到

玫瑰啊,红玫瑰,
　我们向她抛撒,
百合啊,白百合,我们要掷在她的脚下;

The little Queen's coming,

The people are running—

The people are running to greet and to meet.

Then clash out a welcome;

Let all the bells sound, come,

To give her a welcoming proud and sweet.

How her blue eyes will beam,

And her golden curls gleam,

When the sound of our singing rings down the street.

小女王驾到了，
人们在奔跑观望，奔走相告，
只为看见她、急切问候她。

我们欢呼鼓掌，
钟声响彻云霄，
我们以她为傲，喜迎她的驾到。
她蓝色的眼睛多么明亮，
她金色的卷发多么闪耀，
让我们的歌声回响在整个街道。

ON THE WALL TOP

DANCING and prancing to town we go,
On the top of the wall of the town we go.
Shall we talk to the stars, or talk to the moon,
Or run along home to our dinner so soon?

走在城墙上

我们蹦蹦跳跳进城去,
一路沿着城墙顶上走。
我们是先和星星聊,还是与月亮说个悄悄话,
还是赶快回家吃晚饭?

So high — so high on the wall we run,

The nearer the sky — why, the nearer the sun.

If you give me one penny, I'll give you two,

For that's the way good neighbors do.

我们奔跑在高高的城墙上,
蓝天更近,太阳触手可及。
你如果投我以桃,我必报你以李,
礼尚往来才能成为好邻里。

TIP-A-TOE

TIP-A-TOE,
See them go;
One, two, three—
Chloe, Prut, and me.
Up and down,
To the town.
A Lord was there,
And the Lady fair.
And what did they sing?
Oh, "ring-a-ding-ding;"
And the Black Crow flew off
With the Lady's Ring.

踮起脚尖

踮起脚尖,
看她们走路;
一、二、三——
克洛伊,普鲁特和我。
深一脚,浅一脚,
去镇上遛一遛。
那里有个贵族,
还有窈窕淑女。
他们在唱着什么?
哦,"叮——啊——叮——叮";
引来一只乌鸦,
叼着淑女的戒指飞走了。

MAMMAS AND BABIES

"MY Polly is so very good,
And Belinda never cries;
My baby often goes to sleep,
And see how she shuts her eyes."

"Dear Mrs. Lemon tell me when
Belinda goes to school;
And what time does she go to bed?"
"Well, eight o'clock's the rule."

妈妈们和孩子们

"我家的波莉很是乖,
　贝琳达从来不哭闹;
　我的娃娃爱睡觉,
　看她闭着双眼笑。"

"亲爱的雷蒙太太告诉我,
　贝琳达何时去学校;
　还有她几点钟去睡觉?"
"嗯,校规说,八点一到便睡觉。"

"But now and then, just for a treat,
I let her wait a while;
You shake your head — why, wouldn't you?
Do look at Baby's smile!"

"Dear Mrs. Primrose will you come
One day next week to tea?
Of course bring Rosalinda, and
That darling — Rosalie."

"Dear Mrs. Cowslip, you are kind;
My little folks, I know,
Will be so very pleased to come;
Dears, tell Mrs. Cowslip so."

"但时不时,作为奖励,
我会让她晚点上床睡;
你不信?为何把头摇?
看看宝贝的微笑就知道!"

"亲爱的普里姆罗斯太太,
下周找一天来喝茶?
当然要带上罗莎琳达,
还有可爱的罗莎莉。"

"亲爱的考思利普太太,您真善良;
我知道我的这些小家伙,
都巴不得到您那里去;
亲爱的,快告诉考思利普太太,是不是啊!"

"Oh, do you know — perhaps you've not heard —
  She had a dreadful fright;
My Daisy with the measles
  Kept me up every night."

"And then I've been so worried
  Clarissa had a fit:
And the doctor said he couldn't
  In the least account for it."

"哦,你知道吗?也许你还没听说——
但肯定会吓一大跳;
我的戴茜出麻疹了,
让我每晚都睡不着觉。"

"我一直担心会这样——
克拉丽莎果真也出现了症状。
连医生都说不知如何
解决当下的问题。"

MY LITTLE GIRLIE

LITTLE girlie tell to me
What your wistful blue eyes see?
Why you like to stand so high,
Looking at the far-off sky.

我的小姑娘

我的小姑娘请快告诉我，
你忧郁的蓝眼睛在找寻什么？
为什么你要站得那么高，
望着天边的白云飘飘。

Does a tiny Fairy flit
In the pretty blue of it?
Or is it that you hope so soon
To see the rising yellow Moon?

Or is it — as I think I've heard —
You're looking for a little Bird
To come and sit upon a spray,
And sing the summer night away?

是不是有个小仙女,
飞在美丽的蓝天中?
还是你希望,
快快见到升起的黄月亮?

还是像我听到的那样,
你正在寻找一只小小鸟,
飞来坐到近处的枝头上,
伴着它的歌声,夏夜渐渐散去?

THE CATS HAVE COME TO TEA

WHAT did she see — oh, what did she see,
As she stood leaning against the tree?
Why all the Cats had come to tea.

猫咪来喝茶

她看到了啥?哦,她看到了啥?
当她斜靠在大树上?
为什么猫咪都来喝茶了?

What a fine turn out — from round about!
All the houses had let them out,
And here they were with scamper and shout.

"Mew-mew-mew!" was all they could say,
And, "we hope we find you well today."

Oh, what should she do — oh, what should she do?
What a lot of milk they would get through;
For here they were with "mew-mew-mew;"

She didn't know — oh, she didn't know,
If bread and butter they'd like or no;
They might want little mice, oh! Oh! Oh!

Dear me — oh, dear me,
All the cats had come to tea.

四面八方,家家户户,
敲开房门,让猫咪们出来闲逛,
它们蹦蹦跳跳,尖叫发狂。

"喵,喵,喵!"它们齐声叫,
并"祝小姐今天过得好!"

哦,她该怎么办呀?哦,如何是好?
她喂给猫咪们的牛奶该是多少?
"喵,喵,喵"的叫声还没完没了。

她不知道啊,哦,她不知道,
猫咪们也许喜欢黄油和面包?
哦!哦!哦!它们或许觉得小老鼠更好。

我的天啊,哦!我的天,
所有的猫咪都来喝茶了。

THE TEA PARTY

IN the pleasant green Garden
We sat down to tea;
"Do you take sugar?" and
"Do you take milk?"

She'd got a new gown on —
A smart one of silk.
We all were as happy
As happy could be,
On that bright Summer's day
When she asked us to tea.

茶话会

坐在碧草如茵的美丽花园里，
　我们喝着下午茶；
"你要不要加点糖？"
"你要不要加些奶？"
　她穿着新长裙，
　漂亮的丝绸装。
在明媚的夏日里，
她请我们来喝茶。
我们一如既往，
　尽情欢畅。

UNDER ROSE ARCHES

UNDER Rose Arches to Rose Town —
Rose Town on the top of the hill;
For the Summer wind blows and music goes,
And the violins sound shrill.

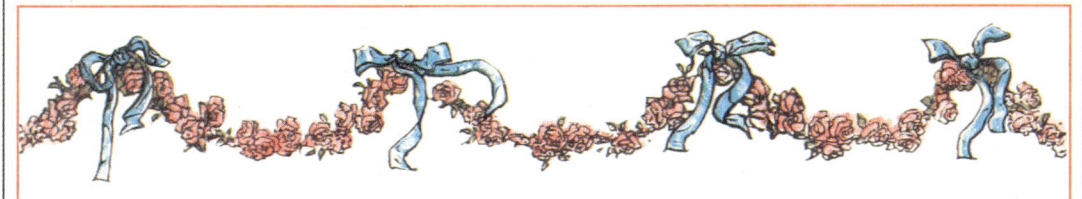

在玫瑰廊下

穿过玫瑰廊就是玫瑰镇,
玫瑰镇坐落在那山顶上;
夏风习习,乐声悠悠,
小提琴的曲调悦耳清扬。

Oh, Roses shall be for her carpet,
And her curtains of Roses so fair;
And a rosy crown, while far adown
Floats her long golden hair.

Twist and twine Roses and Lilies,
And little leaves green,
Fit for a queen;
Twist and twine Roses and Lilies.

Twist and twine Roses and Lilies,
And all the bells ring,
And the people sing;
Twist and twine Roses and Lilies.

哦，用玫瑰花为她铺成地毯，
　她的玫瑰窗帘多么好看；
　她用玫瑰花编成王冠，
　长长的金发飘落下来。

把玫瑰花和百合花拧成花环，
　　中间夹些嫩绿叶，
　　送给女王最合适；
把玫瑰花和百合花拧成花环。

把玫瑰花和百合花拧成花环，
　　钟声全部敲响，
　　人们放声欢唱；
把玫瑰花和百合花拧成花环。

A GENTEEL FAMILY

SOME children are so naughty,
And some are very good;
But the Genteel Family
Did always what it should.

They put on gloves when they went out,
And ran not in the street;
And on wet days not one of them
Had ever muddy feet.

教养之家

有些孩子很淘气，
有些孩子好脾气；
但在教养之家里，
一切都须按家律。

出门要戴上手套，
不能跑着上街道；
雨天一个也不许
满脚泥巴脏兮兮。

Then they were always so polite,
And always thanked you so;
And never threw their toys about,
As naughty children do.

They always learnt their lessons
When it was time they should;
And liked to eat up all their crusts —
They were so very good.

And then their frocks were never torn,
Their tuckers always clean;
And their hair so very tidy —
Always quite fit to be seen.

他们总是优雅有礼，
　对你不停致谢意；
从来不像淘气包，
　到处撒玩具。

他们总是守时间，
　准时上课去学习；
就连面包都吃得巧，
　每次吃光不扔皮。

她们的裙子从不破，
她们的披肩总干净；
她们的头发常打理，
看上去顺眼又得体。

Then they made calls with their mamma,
And were so very neat;
And learnt to bow becomingly
When they met you in the street.

And really they were everything
That children ought to be;
And well may be examples now
For little you and me.

当和妈妈访亲戚，
穿戴干净又整齐；
走在街上遇见你，
鞠躬行礼很得体。

她们一言一行是典范，
都是该养成的好习惯；
也是你我的好榜样，
我们从小学习有教养。

BABY MINE

BABY mine, over the trees;
Baby mine, over the flowers;
Baby mine, over the sunshine;
Baby mine, over the showers.

Baby mine, over the land;
Baby mine, over the water.
Oh, when had a mother before
Such a sweet — such a sweet, little daughter.

我的宝贝

我的宝贝，穿过树木成行，
我的宝贝，细嗅鲜花芬芳；
我的宝贝，拥抱灿烂千阳；
我的宝贝，沐浴美好时光。

我的宝贝，热爱这片土地；
我的宝贝，泛舟溪水海洋。
哦！当妈妈面对如此爱女，
看着小女儿难免心旷神怡。

LITTLE GIRLS AND LITTLE LAMBS

IN the May-time flowers grow;
Little girls in meadows go;
Little lambs frisk with delight,
And in the green grass sleep at night.
Little birds sing all the day,
Oh, in such a happy way!
All the day the sun is bright,
And little stars shine all the night.

小姑娘和小羔羊

五月里的鲜花遍地开,
小姑娘们踏青尽开怀;
小羔羊们在草地上奔跑欢跳,
夜幕降临,绿草地渐渐安详。
小鸟们整日放声歌唱,
哦,这样的一天多欢快!
白天艳阳高照,
夜晚繁星闪耀。

The Cowslip says to the Primrose,
"How soft the little Spring wind blows!"
The Daisy and the Buttercup
Sing every time that they look up.
For beneath the sweet blue sky
They see a pretty Butterfly;
The Butterfly, when he looks down,
Says, "what a pretty Flower Town!"

　　九轮草对报春花低语：
　"春风多么温柔缠绕！"
　　雏菊和毛茛草，
　它们抬起头便唱不休。
　　在湛蓝的天空下，
　一只漂亮的蝴蝶振翅飞翔；
　　蝴蝶俯瞰着大地，
　说："好一座美丽的花乡！"

FROM WONDER WORLD

OUT of Wonder World I think you come,
For in your eyes the wonder comes with you.
The stars are the windows of Heaven,
And sometimes I think you peep through.
Oh, little girl, tell us do the Flowers
Tell you secrets when they find you all alone.
Or the Birds and Butterflies whisper
Of things to us unknown?

来自奇幻的国度

我猜你一定来自奇幻的国度;
因为你的双眼满是迷雾。
星星是通往天国的窗户,
有时我觉得你早已看透。

哦,小姑娘,请告诉我们,
当你独自一人时,花儿和你说了啥?
鸟儿和蝴蝶对你的低声细语,
还有哪些我们不知道?

Or do angel voices speak to you so softly,
When we only hear a little wind sigh?
And the peaceful dew of Heaven fall upon you
When we only see a white cloud passing by?

当我们听见微风轻拂，
难道是天使在与你亲昵低语？
当我们看见白云飘飘，
可是天堂的露珠爱抚于你？

CHILD'S SONG

THE King and the Queen were riding
Upon a Summer's day,
And a Blackbird flew above them
To hear what they did say.

The King said he liked apples,
And the Queen said she liked pears.
And what shall we do to the Blackbird
Who listens unawares.

儿歌

一个炎炎的夏日里,
国王和王后跨上坐骑。
一只乌鸫紧紧跟随,
想听听有什么新奇事儿。

国王说他喜欢苹果,
王后说她偏爱鸭梨。
我们如何处置这只乌鸫,
因为它听到了一个秘密。

MISS MOLLY AND THE LITTLE FISHES

OH, sweet Miss Molly,
You're so fond
Of Fishes in a little Pond.
And perhaps they're glad
To see you stare
With such bright eyes
Upon them there.

茉莉小姐和小鱼儿

哦,可爱的莫莉小姐,
正饶有兴趣地
看着池塘里的小鱼儿,
靓丽的眼睛,瞪得专心至极,
见此情景,小鱼儿乐得不能自已。

And when your fingers and your thumbs
Drop slowly in the small white crumbs,
I hope they're happy. Only this
When you've looked long enough, sweet miss.
Then, most beneficent young giver,
Restore them to their native river.

请你用食指和大拇指
揪几块白面包,慢慢放入水中。
我想小鱼儿一定快乐幸福,
还能让你,这位美丽的小姐看个够。
那么,最慈悲的年轻人啊,
最终请让它们游回源头。

THE LITTLE JUMPING GIRLS

JUMP, jump, jump,

Jump away

From this town into

The next, today.

Jump, jump, jump,

Jump over the moon;

Jump all the morning,

And all the noon.

小女孩,蹦蹦跳

蹦啊跳啊跳,
你能跳到远方;
今天从一个镇子
跳到另一个镇子。

蹦啊跳啊跳,
跳过月亮;
跳过清晨,
跳过正午。

Jump, jump, jump,
Jump all night;
Won't our mothers
Be in a fright?

Jump, jump, jump,
And leave behind
Everything evil
That we may find.

Jump, jump, jump,
Over the sea;
What wonderful wonders
We shall see.

Jump, jump, jump,
Jump far away;
And all come home
Some other day.

蹦啊跳啊跳,
跳过黑夜;
会不会吓到
我们的妈妈?

蹦啊跳啊跳,
跳过我们遭遇的
所有厄运,
不留丝毫。

蹦啊跳啊跳,
跳过大海;
我们将看到
世间奇境多美妙。

蹦啊跳啊跳,
你能跳到远方;
终有一天我们都会回家,
不再蹦跳。

RING-A-RING

RING-A-RING of little boys,
Ring-a-ring of girls;
All around, all around,
Twists and twirls.

You are merry children;
"Yes, we are."
Where do you come from?
"Not very far."

"We live in the mountain,
We live in the tree;
And I live in the river-bed,
And you won't catch me!"

转圆圈

小男孩儿转圆圈。
小女孩儿转圆圈;
转呀转,
一圈又一圈。

你们真是快乐的孩子;
"是的,我们是呀。"
你们打哪儿来呀?
"不是很远的地方呀。"

"我们住在山里,
我们住在树间;
我住在河床边,
你抓不住我的,我很顽皮!"

ON THE BRIDGE

IF I could see a little fish —
That is what I just now wish —
I want to see his threat round eyes
Always open in surprise.

I wish a water-rat would glide
Slowly to the other side,

在桥上

我现在的愿望,
是能看见一条小鱼!
我想看到它那瞪圆的眼睛里,
充满害怕和惊奇。

我希望有一只水鼠溜过,
慢慢划到河的对岸;

Or a dancing spider sit
On the yellow flags a hit.
I think I'll get some stones to throw
And watch the pretty circles show.
Or shall we sail a flower-boat.
And watch it slowly, slowly float?

That's nice because you never know
How far away it means to go;
And when tomorrow comes, you see,
It may be in the great wide sea.

也希望一直舞蹈的蜘蛛，
偶尔坐在黄旗子上换口气。

我想向水中投些石子，
看掀起的一圈圈涟漪。
或者让我们泛一叶花舟，
观其慢慢地顺流而去？

很奇妙，因为你永不知道，
它会漂得多远，在下一秒；
试想，明日的这个时候，
或许它已融入大海的怀抱。

BALL

ONE, two, is one to you;
One, two, three, is one to me.
Throw it fast or not at all,
And mind you do not let it fall.

抛球

一、二,球先扔给你;
一、二、三,球再传给我!
　　快慢你随意,
　　别让它落地。

Fairy Blue Eyes,

And Fairy Brown,

And dear little Golden Curls,

Look down.

I say "goodbye"

"Goodbye" with no pain —

Till some happy day

We meet again!

蓝眼睛的小精灵,
和棕眼睛的小精灵,
还有可爱的金发毛毛卷,
注意了,
我要说"再见",
"再见"并非遗憾,
在某个欢乐的日子里,
我们还会再相见!

译后记

童心未泯的绘本创作者

凯特·格林威（Kate Greenaway，1846—1901），是英国19世纪最具影响力的童书插画家之一，甚至与创作《青蛙求偶记》(*A Frog He Would A-Wooing Go*)的蓝道夫·凯迪克（Randolph Caldecott）、绘制《睡美人》(*The Sleeping Beauty*)的沃尔特·克莱恩（Walter Crane）并称为"英国绘本三巨头"，他们三人大大地改变了现代图画书的表现形式，更引领了英国绘本的黄金发展时期。

凯特·格林威

成长于英国乡村的纯真之心

1846年，凯特·格林威出生于伦敦的雷克斯顿区（Hoxton）。因为父亲是一名绘图员和雕版印刷师，当格林威刚学会握笔的时候，父亲就鼓励她开始画画。稍长之后的格林威除了画画之外，也非常喜欢装饰自己的洋娃娃，小小年纪就展现出她对艺术的喜爱。12岁时，她进入皇家女子艺术学校（Royal Female School of Art）学习装饰艺术；之后就读于希瑟利艺术学校（Heatherley School of Fine Art），并在22岁时举办了她人生中的第一场水彩画展。

16岁的凯特·格林威

格林威在一个叫作罗雷斯顿（Rolleston）的小村庄度过了其童年的大段时光，她曾经说过："当我还是个孩子时，在乡间度过了非常快乐的时光。"乡村的老式英国风情和童年的愉快记忆对她的绘画风格产生了很大的影响，从她的作品中可以发现，画作里充满了浪漫的氛围，场景大多在田野、花园、牧场或是小村庄，笔下的人物则以女性和孩童为主。仔细评析格林威的画作可以发现，她强调细节，用色鲜明强烈，有其独特的纤细之美。

19 世纪末的格林威风潮

19 世纪 70 年代，英国有一位知名的木刻印刷师埃德蒙·埃文斯（Edmund Evans），他改善了彩色印刷的技术，大大提升了原本低劣的图画书品质，同时他也不断地挖掘优秀的插画家，并一同合作，共同出版图画书。格林威原本专为节庆贺卡绘制插图，埃文斯相中了她的风格，认为十分符合当时维多利亚时代的大众口味，便邀请她创作了格林威人生的第一本图画书——《窗下》（Under the Window）。

埃文斯曾说，当他一读完《窗下》的诗文和插图草稿之后，便深深为之着迷，于是他马上说服出版商出版此书，在首印时就大手笔地印了两万本，这在当时是相当庞大的印量。不过读者的反应证明了埃文斯的眼光没错，《窗下》果然大受欢迎，上市后便售罄，后足足加印了五万本。前前后后更再版多次，于格林威一生当中，总共销售超过十万本，相继翻译成德文、法文、日文等多国语言，着实成为了时代经典。

因为《窗下》在商业上的成功，插画中的人物穿着常被人拿

凯特·格林威的服装设计风格

来讨论研究。格林威笔下人物的服饰参照了18世纪末至19世纪初的穿着风格，虽然在格林威生活的19世纪末，这种风格被认为有些过时，但19世纪下半叶正处于欧洲的艺术服饰运动（Artistic Dress Movement），主张拒绝高度复杂僵硬的穿衣风格，兴起使用更为简洁的设计；同时也受到前拉斐尔派的艺术风格影响，让格林威笔下的服饰重新流行起来。因此，格林威成了一个家喻户晓的名字，甚至在当时掀起了一股格林威风潮（Greenaway Vogue）。

与同时期崭露头角的凯迪克即克莱恩相比较，格林威的作品从女性视角出发，风格较为细腻优美，她笔下的人物穿着18世纪后期流行的服饰，例如镶有花边的礼袍、头上和腰间都系着丝带；文字更多着眼于美好纯真的时光，关注孩子的天真烂漫、纯真朴实的心灵，与同时期的其他两位插画家的风格有着明显不同。

余音绕梁的经典

格林威大部分作品的文字都来自民间耳熟能详的歌谣，例如《鹅妈妈童谣》（*Mother Goose*）、《金盏花花园》（*Marigold Garden*）、《小安》（*Little Ann*）、《四月儿歌》（*April Baby's Book of Tunes*）、《儿童生日书》（*Kate Greenaway's Birthday Book for Children*）以及《苹果派》（*Apple Pie*）皆是以童谣改编而成。

1855年，为了纪念格林威对插画领域的贡献，英国图书馆协会（The Library Association）以她的名字创办了"凯特·格林威奖"（The CILIP Kate Greenaway Medal），此奖是英国历史最悠久并且最重要的绘本奖项，评选标准包含了艺术风格、格式、图文整合与视觉印象，对于插画的严格审视，让格林威奖在国际上有着极高的声誉，至今仍是许多插画家、作家角逐的绘本大奖。

无数英国孩子是在格林威插画的童书陪伴下长大的,有些甚至受到她的绘画风格影响,成为著名的插画家,如以花仙子系列作品(*Flower Fairies*)闻名的巴克(Cicely Mary Barker)就是其中一个例子。即使一百多年过去了,格林威的作品依然为全世界的读者喜爱着,每一次翻阅都能碰上可爱的孩子与风景,感受属于那个时代的艺术氛围,相信不论是大人或是孩子,都可以在这些经典图画书中获得美感和乐趣。

凯特·格林威故居,位于英国伦敦汉普斯特德,
由英国著名建筑师理查德·肖设计建造

记录美好的童年

《金盏花花园》(*Marigold Garden*)首版于1885年出版上市,也是一本上市即畅销的儿歌经典,格林威秉持一贯的绘画风格,线条细腻,色彩艳丽饱和,人物形象更加丰富多彩,动态图占比增多,主要跟儿歌主题休戚相关。儿歌多涉及儿童日常生活、游戏、习惯养成、教养等,也留下了很多经典的诗句。格林威为本书精选了40首诗歌,如《小小蓝鞋子》《雏菊》《和奶奶一起散步》《当你和我长大》《致太阳门》《伦敦小姑娘》《小女王驾到》《教养之家》等,读起来朗朗上口不说,诗意浪漫无限,诗境美感十足。

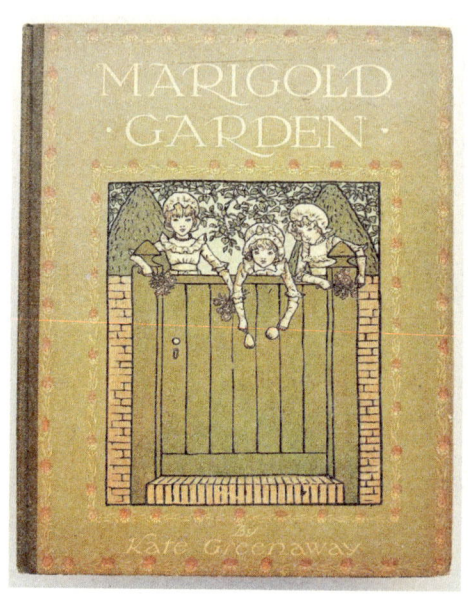
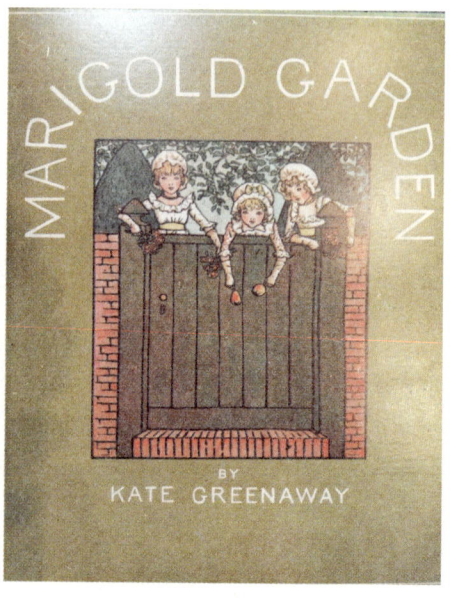

图书在版编目（CIP）数据

金盏花花园：英汉对照 /（英）凯特·格林威
（Kate Greenaway）著绘；繁多译. —沈阳：辽宁人民
出版社，2024.7
（"世界儿童经典插图版"丛书）
ISBN 978-7-205-10828-1

Ⅰ.①金… Ⅱ.①凯… ②繁… Ⅲ.①儿童故事—图画故事—英国—现代 Ⅳ.①I561.85

中国国家版本馆 CIP 数据核字（2023）第 156869 号

出版发行：辽宁人民出版社
　　地址：沈阳市和平区十一纬路 25 号　邮编：110003
　　电话：024-23284321（邮　购）　024-23284324（发行部）
　　传真：024-23284191（发行部）　024-23284304（办公室）
　　http://www.lnpph.com.cn

印　　刷：辽宁新华印务有限公司
幅面尺寸：180mm×210mm
印　　张：6.5
字　　数：70千字
出版时间：2024 年 7 月第 1 版
印刷时间：2024 年 7 月第 1 次印刷
责任编辑：阎伟萍　孙　雯
装帧设计：留白文化
责任校对：冯　莹
书　　号：ISBN 978-7-205-10828-1
定　　价：69.00元